LEVEL 2 READER

Hot Rod Hamster
AND THE HAUNTED
HALLOWEEN PARTY!

WALLINGFORD PUBLIC LIBRARY
200 North Main Street
Wallingford, CT 06492

By Cynthia Lord

Cover illustration by Derek Anderson

Interior illustrations by Greg Paprocki

SCHOLASTIC INC.

CHILDREN'S LIBRARY

To Emily. — C. L.

For my grandparents, Walter and Margaret Schwab,
who always had treats! — D. A.

Text copyright © 2015 by Cynthia Lord
Illustrations copyright © 2015 by Derek Anderson
This book is being published simultaneously in hardcover by Scholastic Press.
All rights reserved. Published by Scholastic Inc., *Publishers since 1920*. SCHOLASTIC, SCHOLASTIC PRESS, and
associated logos are trademarks and/or registered trademarks of Scholastic Inc.
The publisher does not have any control over and does not assume any responsibility for author or third-party
websites or their content.
No part of this publication may be reproduced, stored in a retrieval system, or transmitted in any form or by
any means, electronic, mechanical, photocopying, recording, or otherwise, without written permission of the
publisher. For information regarding permission, write to Scholastic Inc., Attention: Permissions Department,
557 Broadway, New York, NY 10012.

LIBRARY OF CONGRESS CATALOGING-IN-PUBLICATION DATA
Lord, Cynthia, author.
Hot Rod Hamster and the haunted Halloween party / by Cynthia Lord ; cover illustration by Derek Anderson ;
interior illustrations by Greg Paprocki. — First edition.   pages cm
Summary: Hot Rod Hamster is invited to a Halloween party, and he enlists the help of a group of ghosts to win
the spookiest costume contest.
ISBN 978-0-545-81528-4
1. Hamsters—Juvenile fiction. 2. Halloween costumes—Juvenile fiction. 3. Halloween—Juvenile fiction.
4. Contests—Juvenile fiction. 5. Parties—Juvenile fiction. [1. Hamsters—Fiction. 2. Costume—Fiction. 3. Ghosts
—Fiction. 4. Halloween—Fiction. 5. Contests—Fiction. 6. Parties—Fiction.] I. Anderson, Derek, 1969–illustrator.
II. Paprocki, Greg, illustrator. III. Title.   PZ7.L87734Houk 2015   813.6—dc23   [E]   2014038852

10 9 8 7 6 5 4 3 2   15 16 17 18 19/0

Printed in Malaysia   108
First printing 2015

The display type was set in Ziggy ITC and Coop Black.
The text was set in Cochin Medium and Gill Sans Bold.
The interior art was created digitally by Greg Paprocki.
Art direction and book design by Marijka Kostiw

It was Halloween. Hot Rod Hamster hurried off to find his friend Dog. He was on the run to show Dog something fun.

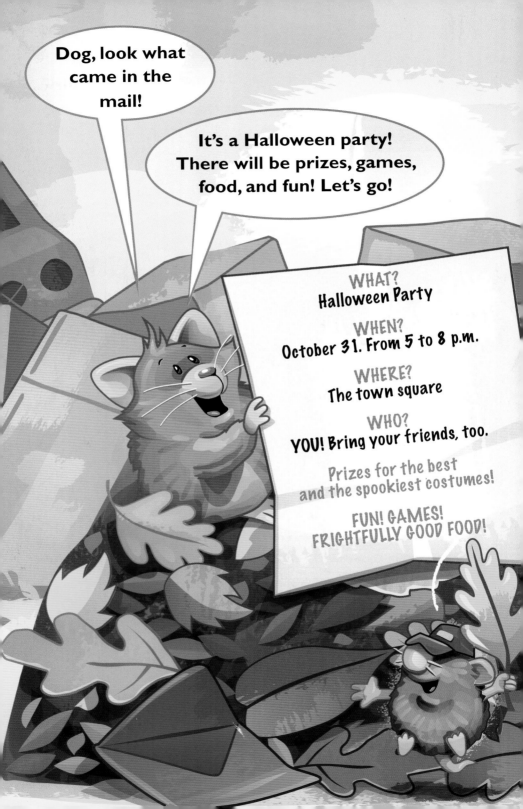

Ghost fun. Clown fun.
Star fun. Crown fun.

Which would *you* choose?

Shake it.

Drum it.

Blow it.

Strum it.

Which would _you_ choose?

Dog builds a stage.
Hamster makes it glow.
Mice add some glitz.
Almost time to go!

HALLOWEEN STUFF

Dog tries to help Hamster with his song.
Mice dream of fun, but—oh no!
Something's wrong.

Dog isn't sure, but Hamster steps inside . . .

Carve time?

Sweet time?

Drink time?

Meet time?

Which would *you* choose?

Dog carves pumpkins.
Hamster tastes the brew.

Ghosts float around
and practice saying "Boo!"

RIP

Boo!

It's time for the
costume judging!
Everyone get
ready!

Mice take their spots,
backup singers, too.